NEW HAVEN PUBLIC

W9-AJP-957

For Mike, Lulu & James - W.A.

Text and design copyright © 2001 by The Templar Company plc
Illustrations copyright © 2001 by Wayne Anderson
All rights reserved.

CIP Data is available.

Published in the United States 2001 by Dutton Children's Books,
a division of Penguin Putnam Books for Young Readers
345 Hudson Street, New York, New York 10014
www.penguinputnam.com

Originally published in Great Britain 2001 by Templar Publishing,
an imprint of The Templar Company plc, Surrey, Great Britain
Designed by Mike Jolley
Edited by A. J. Wood
Printed in Belgium
4 6 8 10 9 7 5 3

First American Edition
ISBN 0-525-46787-4

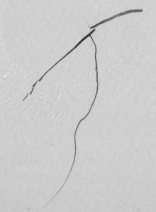

CHILDREN'S ROOM

The Tin Forest

by Helen Ward   illustrated by Wayne Anderson

Dutton Children's Books
New York

There was once a wide, windswept place,

E
WARD

near nowhere and close to forgotten,
that was filled with all the things
that no one wanted.

Right in the middle was a small house,
with small windows,
that looked out on other people's garbage
and bad weather.

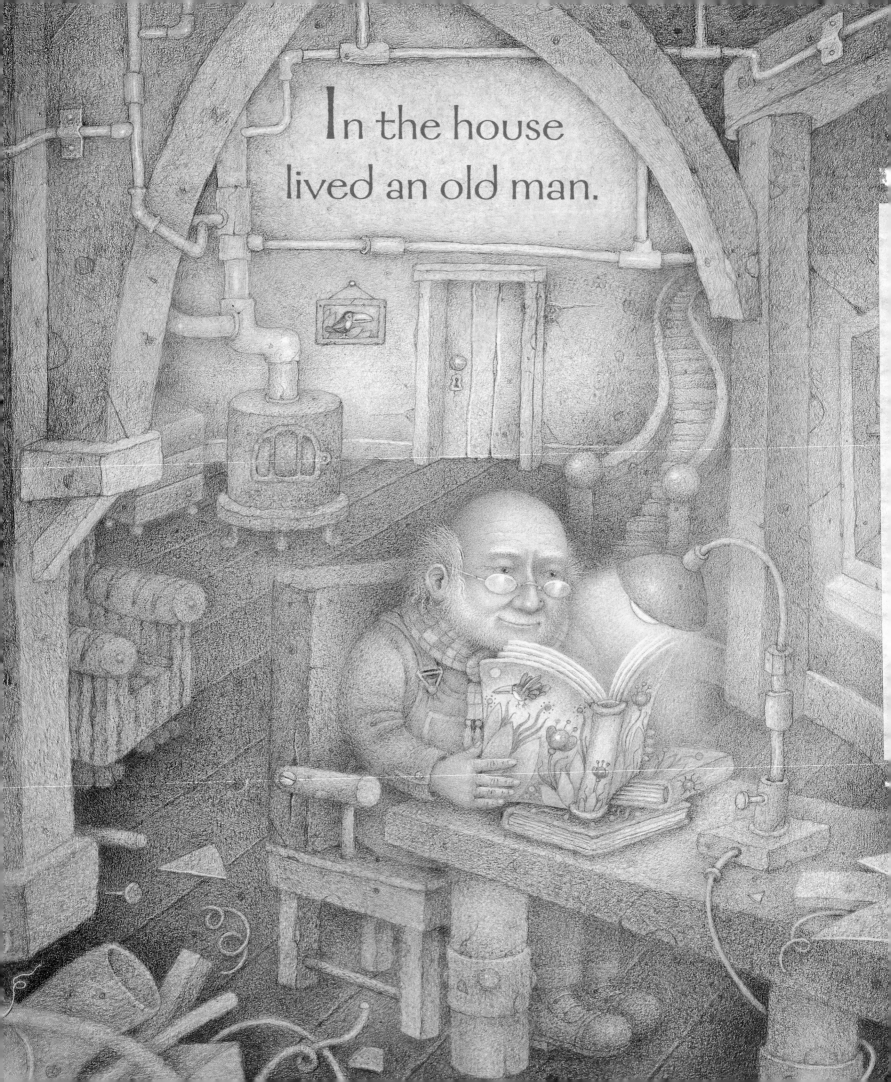

In the house
lived an old man.

Every day he tried to clear away the garbage,

sifting and sorting,

burning and burying.

And every night
the old man
dreamed.

He dreamed he lived in
a forest full of wild animals.
There were colorful birds,
tropical trees, exotic flowers,
toucans, tree frogs,
and tigers.

But when he awoke,
the world outside was
still the same.

One day something
caught the old man's eye,
and an idea planted itself in his mind.

The idea grew roots and sprouted.
Feeding on the garbage,
it grew leaves.

It grew branches.

It grew bigger and bigger.

Under the old man's hand,
a forest emerged.

A forest made of garbage.
A forest made of tin.
It was not the forest of his dreams,
but it was a forest just the same.

Then one day across the barren plain,
the wind swept a small bird.
The old man spilled crumbs from his
sandwich onto the ground.
The bird ate the crumbs and perched
to sing in the branches of a tin tree.

But the next morning, the visitor
was gone.

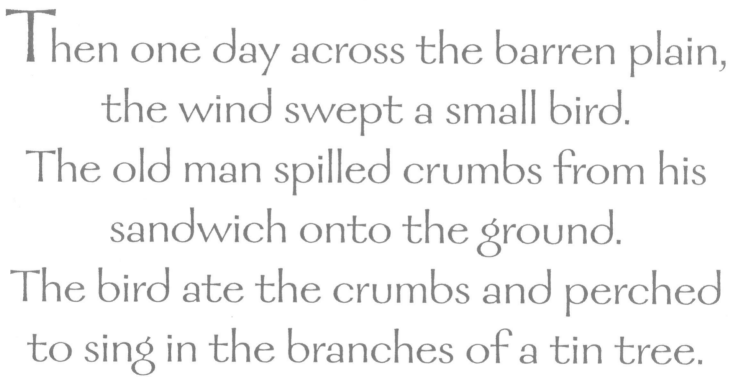

All day the old man
walked through the silence,
and his heart ached with emptiness.

That night, by moonlight,
he made a wish....

In the morning the old man
woke to the sound of birdsong.
The visitor had returned, and his mate
had come with him.
The birds carried seeds in their beaks.
They dropped them to the dry ground.
Green shoots broke through the earth.

Soon the song of birds
mingled with the buzzing of insects
and the rustle of leaves. Time passed.

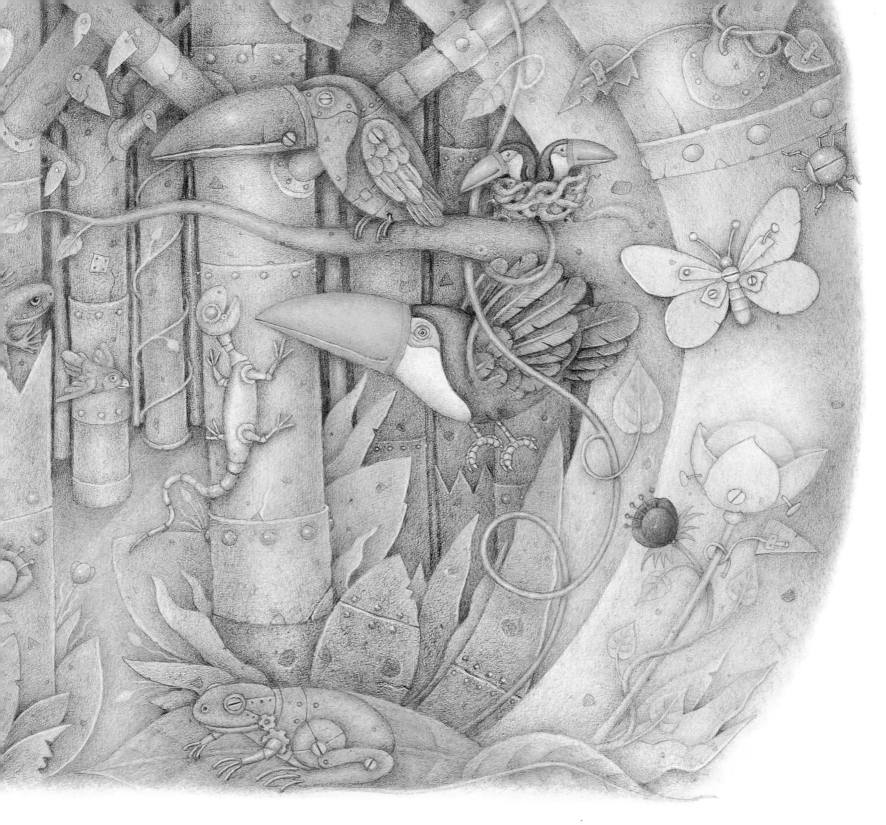

Small creatures appeared, creeping among the forest of trees. Wild animals slipped through the green shadows.

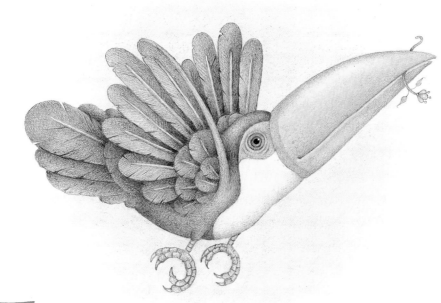

There was once a forest,
near nowhere and close to forgotten,
that was filled with all the things
that everyone wanted.

Right in the middle was a small house,
with small windows. And in the house
lived an old man who never
stopped dreaming.